·I CAN DRAW!·

Dogs & Puppies

EMILY FELLAH

Brimming with creative inspiration, how-to projects, and useful information to enrich your everyday life, Quarto Knows is a favorite destination for those pursuing their interests and passions. Visit our site and dig deeper with our books into your area of interest: Quarto Creates, Quarto Cooks, Quarto Homes, Quarto Lives, Quarto Drives, Quarto Explores, Quarto Gifts, or Quarto Kids.

Walter Foster Jr. titles are also available at discount for retail, wholesale, promotional, and bulk purchase. For details, contact the Special Sales Manager by email at specialsales@quarto.com or by mail at The Quarto Group, Attn: Special Sales Manager, 100 Cummings Center, Suite 265D, Beverly, MA 01915, USA.

ISBN: 978-1-60058-962-1

Digital edition published in 2021
eISBN: 978-1-60058-963-8

Printed in China
10 9 8 7 6 5 4 3 2 1

TABLE OF CONTENTS

HOW TO USE THIS BOOK

Step-by-Step Drawing

This book contains 15 fun drawing projects with step-by-step instructions. Each new step is in color, making it easy to follow along.

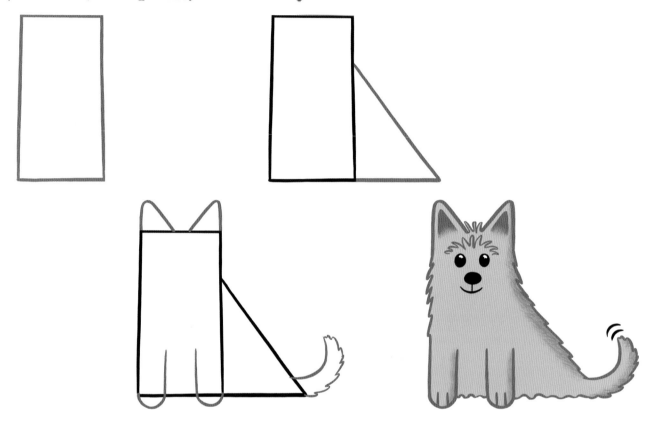

Top Tips

Start lightly in pencil because you will be erasing some of the lines that helped to build your character.

Be careful when erasing because you don't want to crumple or tear your drawing.

If you'd like, you can draw over your finished characters with a fine-line pen or felt-tip marker and erase your pencil lines when the ink is dry.

Tools & Materials

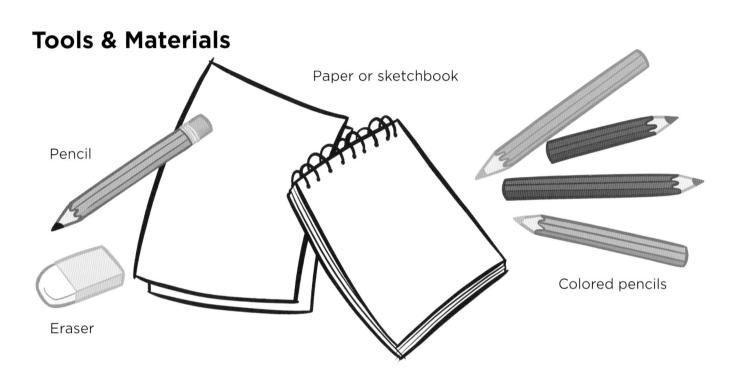

Paper or sketchbook

Pencil

Eraser

Colored pencils

Extras Fine-line pen or felt-tip marker, colored pens, crayons

You Are an Artist!

Your drawings will turn out a little differently from the ones in the book, which is a good thing. You are an individual, and your art will reflect your style and personality, so be proud of it!

GERMAN SHEPHERD

1

2

3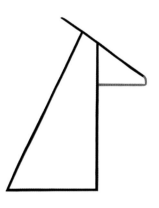

There are a lot of triangular shapes to make when drawing this dog.

4

5

6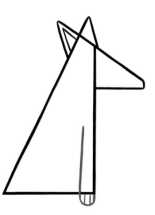

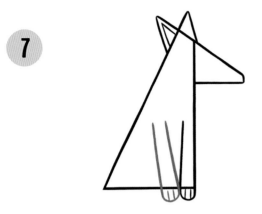

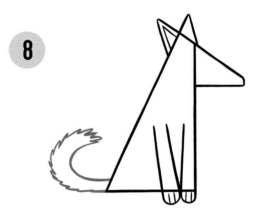

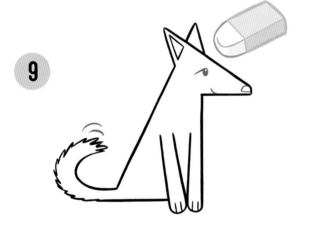

Start with pale orange for the base color, add some pattern in brown, and complete the coloring with some black patches.

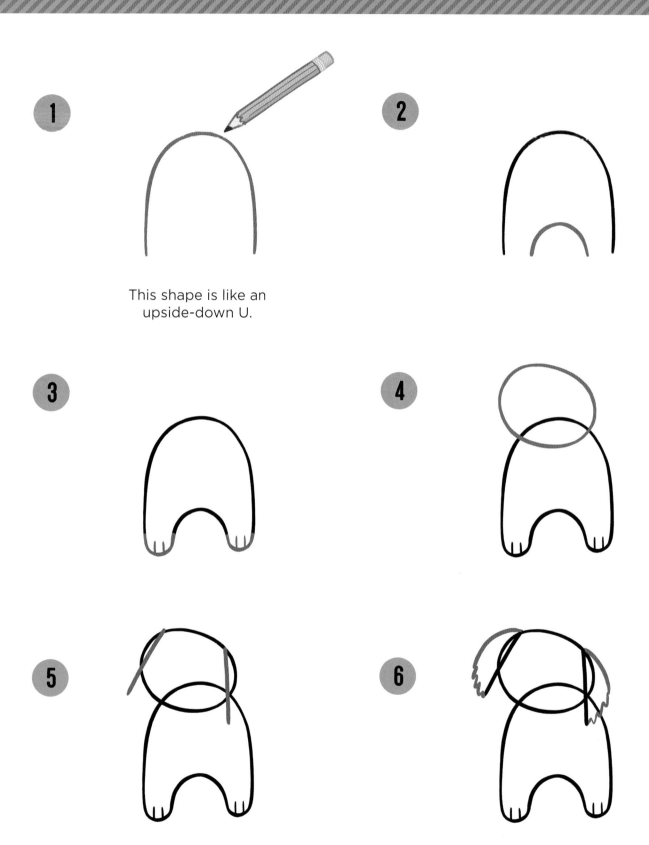

1

This shape is like an upside-down U.

2

3

4

5

Straight lines make up the first part of the ears.

6

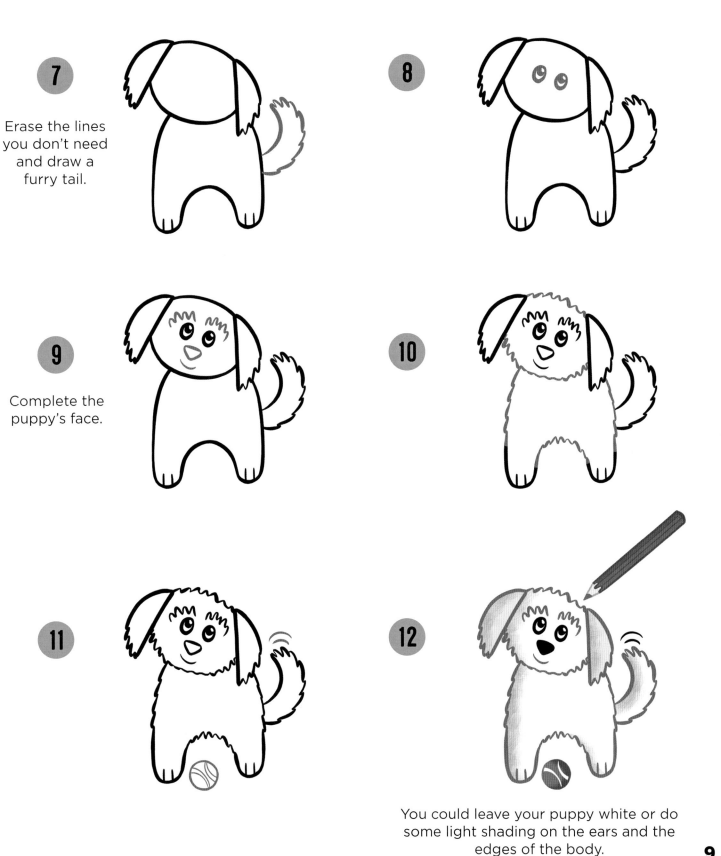

7 Erase the lines you don't need and draw a furry tail.

8

9 Complete the puppy's face.

10

11

12 You could leave your puppy white or do some light shading on the ears and the edges of the body.

9

BASENJI

1

2

3

Take your time to get the
face shape right.

4

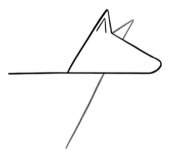

5

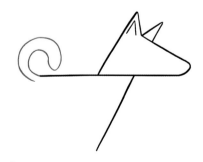

Basenjis have very curly tails.

6

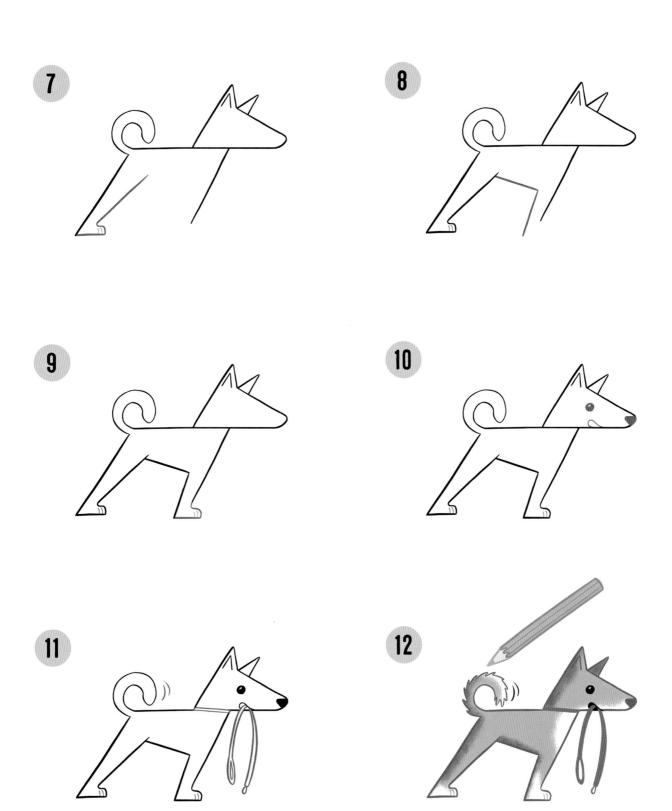

Add the final touches: a leash, collar, and lines by the tail to show that it's wagging.

1
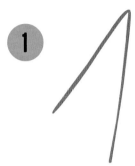

2
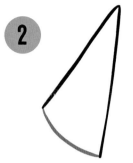

3
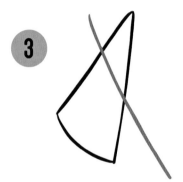

Take your time to position this line.

4
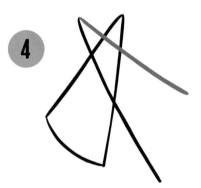

Your dog should now have two ears.

5
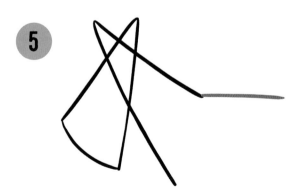

6
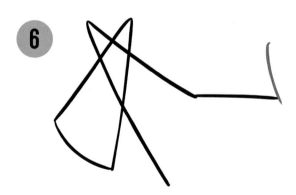

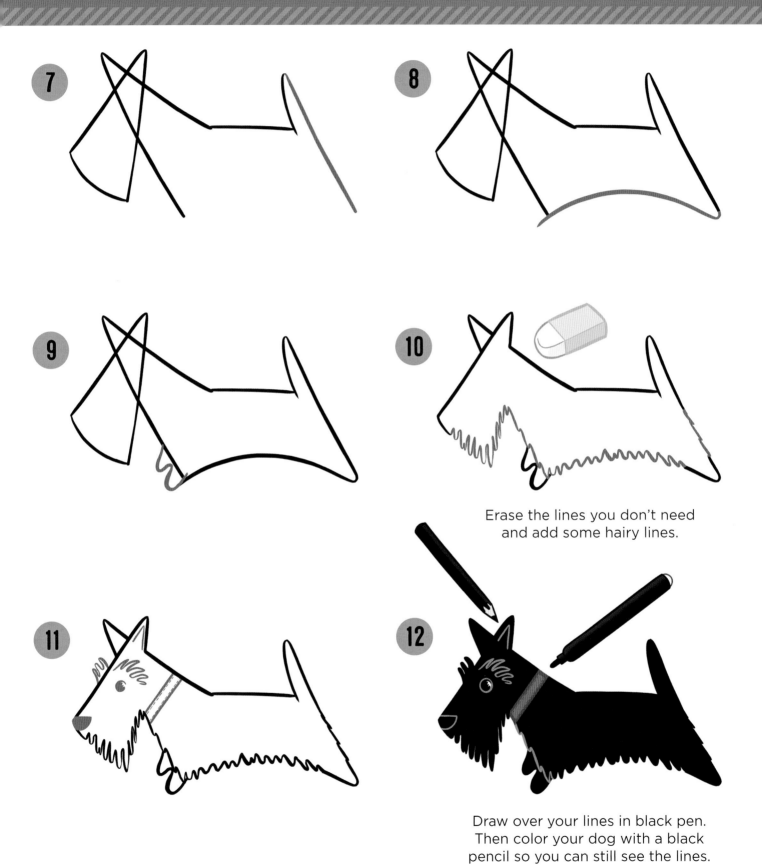

Erase the lines you don't need and add some hairy lines.

Draw over your lines in black pen. Then color your dog with a black pencil so you can still see the lines.

HUSKY PUPPY

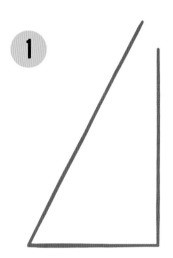

1 Draw a slim triangle with a space at the top.

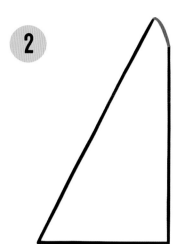

2 Now the space becomes an ear.

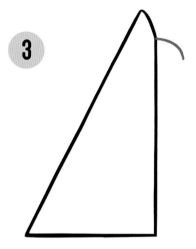

3

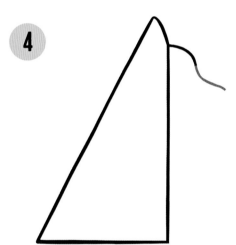

4

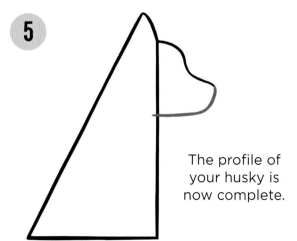

5 The profile of your husky is now complete.

6

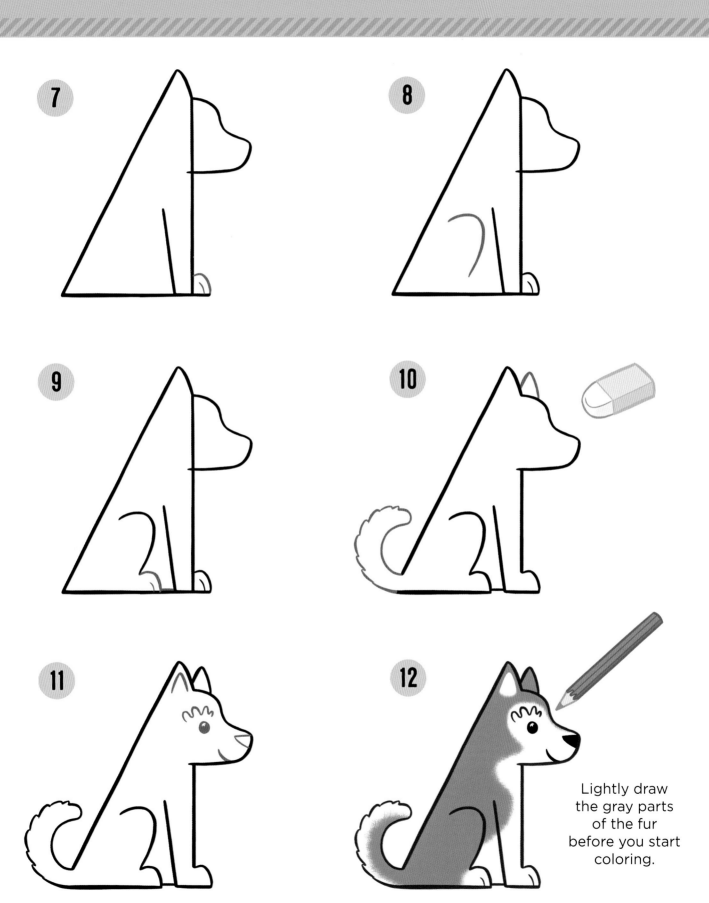

7

8

9

10

11

12

Lightly draw the gray parts of the fur before you start coloring.

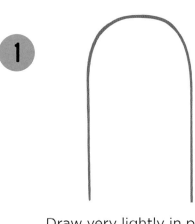

1

Draw very lightly in pencil. You won't want dark pencil lines to show through after adding color.

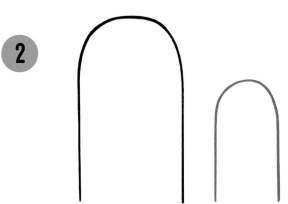

2

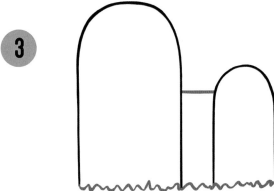

3

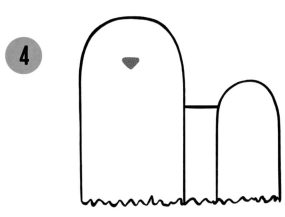

4

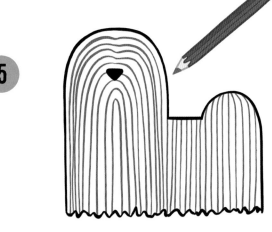

5

Draw the fur lines in brown or cream.

6

Draw over the outer lines to make them look furry.

1

Take your time with this tricky shape.

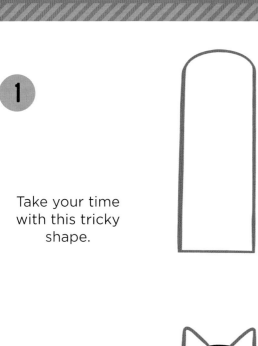

2

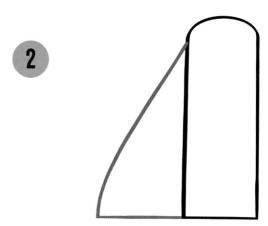

3

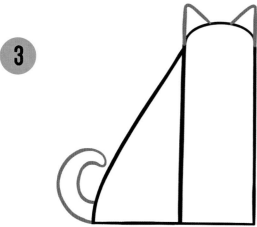

4

5

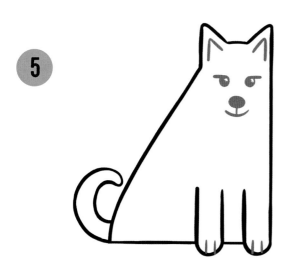

6

Color lightly with an orange pencil, leaving the chest and ears white.

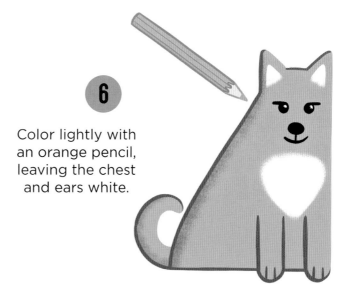

DALMATIAN PUPPY

1 Begin by drawing a circle for the head and a straight line to begin the leg.

2

3

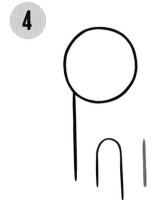

4

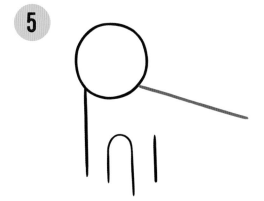

5 Make this body line nice and long.

6

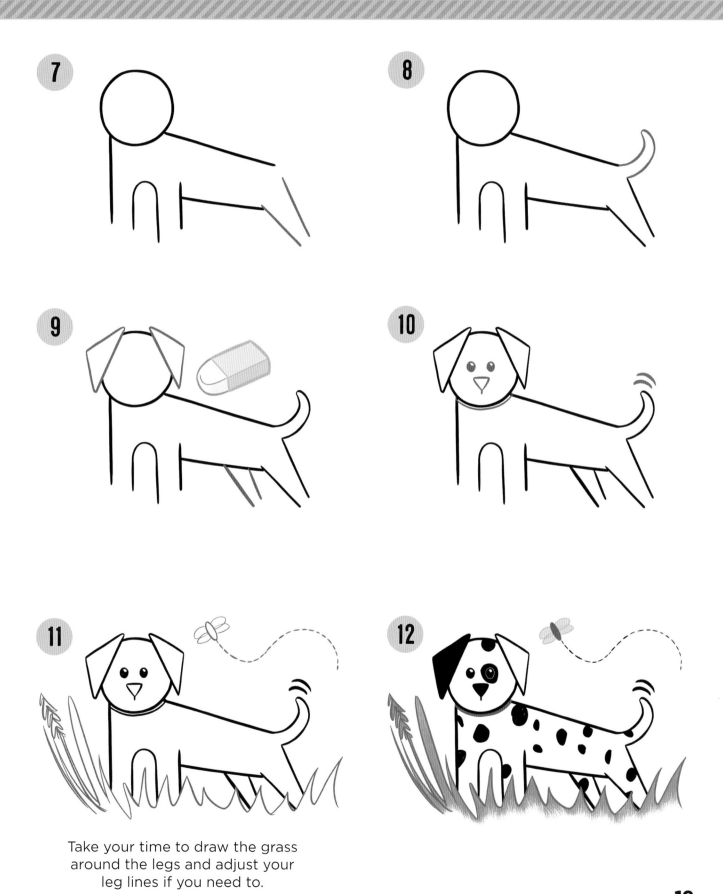

Take your time to draw the grass
around the legs and adjust your
leg lines if you need to.

BULLDOG

The first two shapes are like upside-down U shapes.

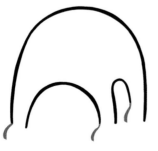

The main part of the bulldog's body is done!

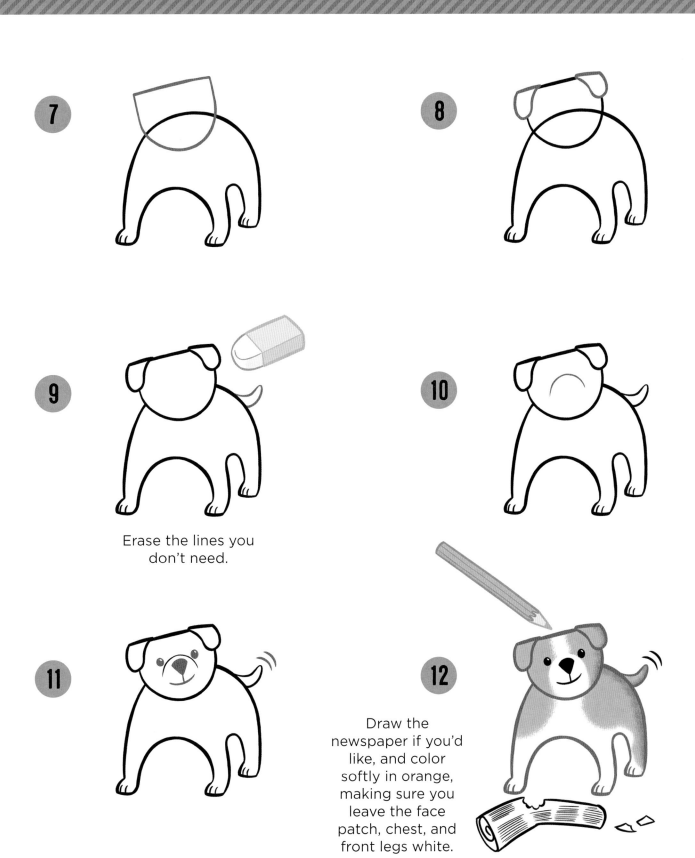

7

8

9

Erase the lines you don't need.

10

11

12

Draw the newspaper if you'd like, and color softly in orange, making sure you leave the face patch, chest, and front legs white.

YORKSHIRE TERRIER PUPPY

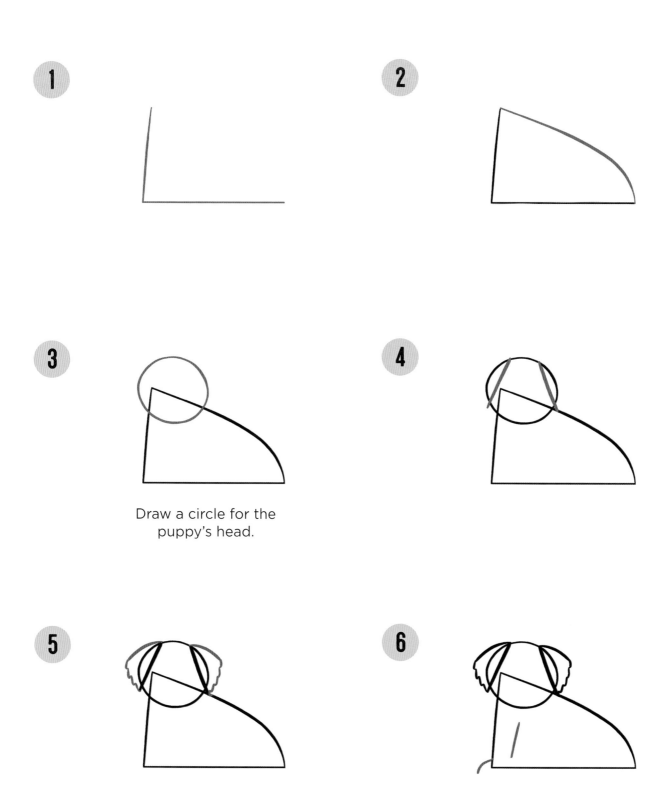

1

2

3

Draw a circle for the puppy's head.

4

5

6

7

Take your time to get the angle of this leg just right.

8

9

10

11

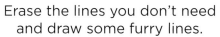

Erase the lines you don't need and draw some furry lines.

12

Great job! Now add some color.

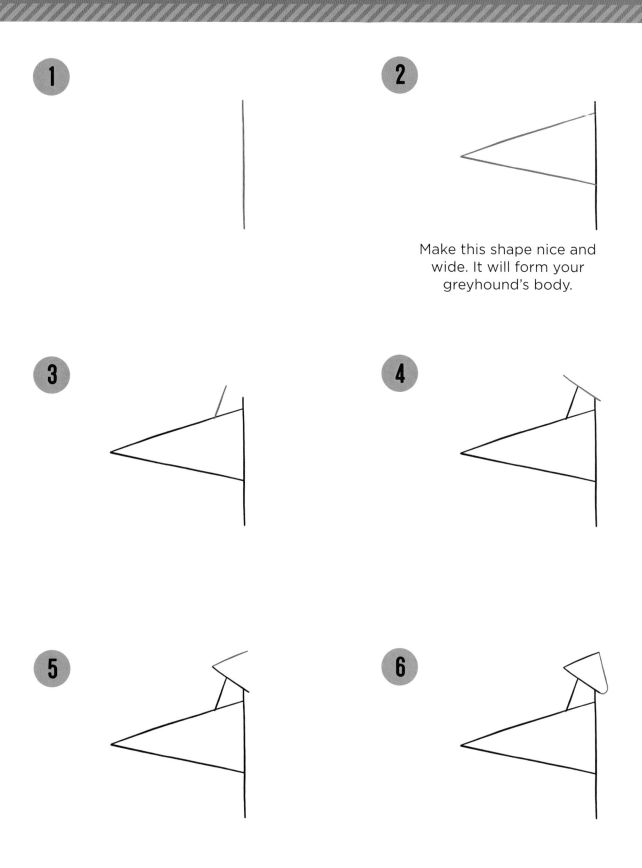

1

2

Make this shape nice and wide. It will form your greyhound's body.

3

4

5

6

7

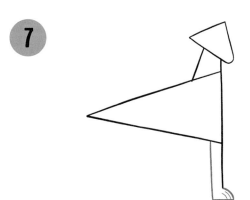

8

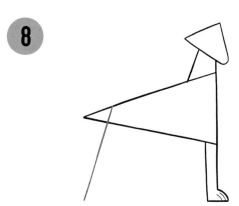

Take care to start this line in the correct position. This will be the greyhound's back leg.

9

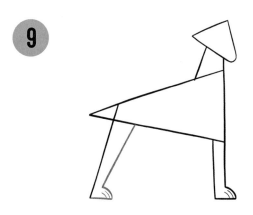

10

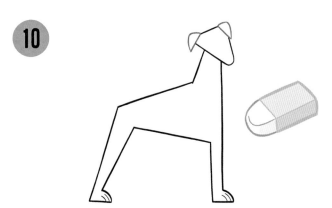

11

12

Color softly in gray, making sure you leave some white patches.

CAIRN TERRIER

1 Start lightly in pencil.

2

3

4 Erase the lines you don't need and draw some furry lines. Cairn terriers have long, shaggy hair.

5

6

POMERANIAN PUPPY

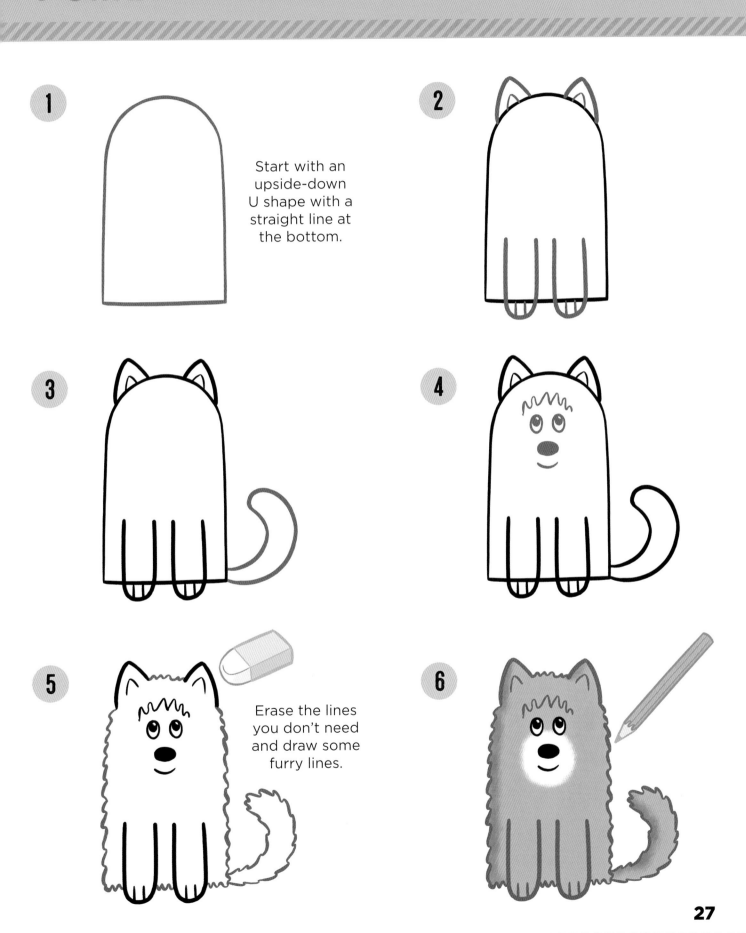

1

Start with an upside-down U shape with a straight line at the bottom.

2

3

4

5

Erase the lines you don't need and draw some furry lines.

6

1

This dog starts with a triangle shape.

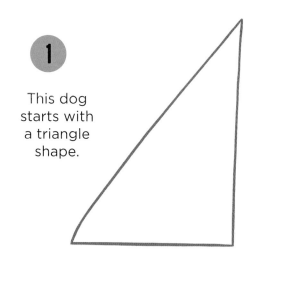

2

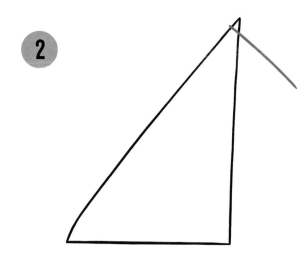

3

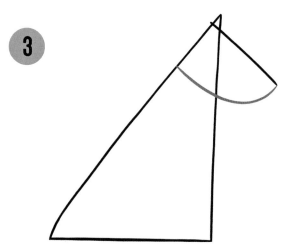

4

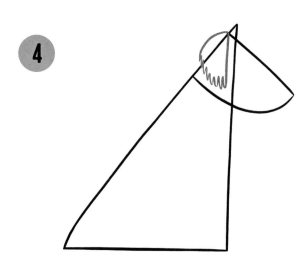

5

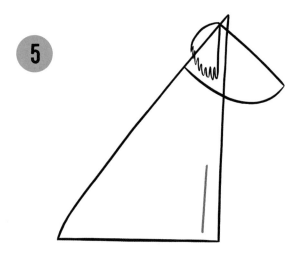

6

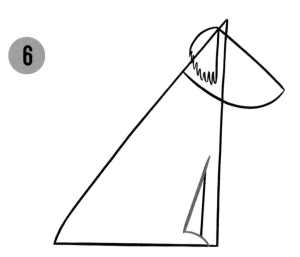

10 Erase the lines you no longer need and draw some furry lines.

The lines in steps 3, 4, and
5 will create the ears.

7 Take your time with the shape of the paws.

8

9

10

11

12 Color your Labrador and draw lots of thin lines on the ears in a darker color.

Also available in this series ...

I Can Draw: Wild Animals
ISBN: 978-1-60058-938-6

I Can Draw: Favorite Pets
ISBN: 978-1-60058-939-3

I Can Draw: Cats & Kittens
ISBN: 978-1-60058-958-4

I Can Draw: Everything Cute & Cuddly
ISBN: 978-1-60058-960-7

Inspiring | Educating | Creating | Entertaining

Visit www.QuartoKnows.com